High as a Hawk

To my big brother, Jim, who led me up my first mountains. —T.A.B.

To Tom, Denali, Brooks and Ben, for getting me up (and down) the mountain. —T.L.

Patricia Lee Gauch, editor

Text copyright © 2004 by Thomas A. Barron.   Illustrations copyright © 2004 by Ted Lewin.
Published simultaneously in Canada.   Manufactured in China by South China Printing Co. Ltd.   Designed by Semadar Megged.
Text set in 16-point Adobe Jenson Semibold.   The illustrations are rendered in watercolor.
Library of Congress Cataloging-in-Publication Data Barron, T. A.   High as a hawk : a brave girl's historic climb / by T. A. Barron ; illustrated by Ted Lewin.
p. cm.   Summary: In 1905, eight-year-old Harriet Peters fulfills her dead mother's dream by climbing Longs Peak in Colorado with the help of an old mountain
guide, Enos Mills. Based on a true story. [1. Longs Peak (Colo.)—Fiction. 2. Mountaineering—Fiction. 3. Mothers and daughters—Fiction. 4. Mills, Enos
Abijah, 1870–1922—Fiction.] I. Lewin, Ted, ill. II. Title. PZ7.B27567 St 2004 [E]—dc22 2003012405
ISBN 0-399-23704-6   10 9 8 7 6 5 4 3 2 1
First Impression

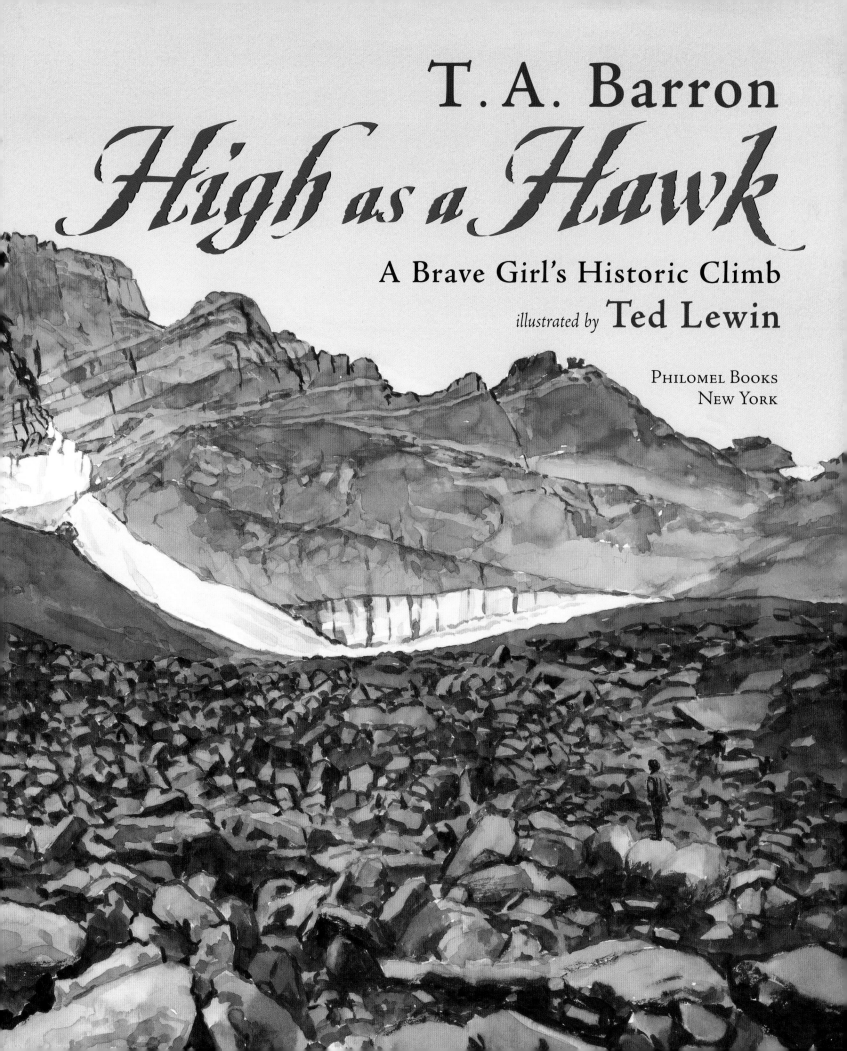

T. A. Barron

High as a Hawk

A Brave Girl's Historic Climb

illustrated by Ted Lewin

PHILOMEL BOOKS
NEW YORK

*D*arkness covered me like a heavy quilt. I could barely see my horse's ears, or the horses of my pa and Mr. Mills, riding beside me. I could only hear—the hooves clomping, that old owl hooting, and sometimes Pa coughing.

Then, between the spruce branches, I saw something—the very top of Longs Peak, glowing in the sunrise. The whole mountain looked pinker than a ripened peach. And big, too.

Way too big to climb.

I thought back to my first climb with Ma, last year in the Ozarks. It was really just a hill, but when I finally reached the top, I felt just as high as the hawk soaring over our heads. Ma laughed out loud, watching me spread my arms wide like wings.

That's when she told me her dream: to climb Longs Peak in Colorado. With Enos Mills, the famous mountain guide who loved that place so much, he wanted to make it a national park. And best of all, she told me that Pa was going to take her there for her next birthday.

She just didn't tell me she was going to die first.

We tied up the horses at the trailhead, and I glanced up at the peak. Lord, it was high! Here I was, just eight years old, half the age of anyone who'd ever climbed it. But I still wanted to try . . . and not just for me. Then Mr. Mills tapped my shoulder. " 'Tis a rough climb for a wee lass," he said, purring like a Scottish cat. "And full of surprises."

I swallowed. And wondered what sort of surprises he meant.

Right away, the trail started climbing.
Up, up, up. Steeper than my attic stairs! I slid
on the frosty grass and scraped both my knees.
Then I tried to hold on to a bush and got a fistful
of thorns. At last I rested by a tree, breathing heavy as
an old mule. My sides ached, my knees throbbed. Up
ahead, Pa was coughing. Why couldn't Ma have picked something easier?
The peak winked at me through the branches. It glowed bright,
with golden light dripping down its sides like honey. And somehow my

Hand over hand, we pulled ourselves up a cliff wall. Rocks broke off and clattered to the bottom. Pa took forever to get up—and when he did, his face looked whiter than aspen bark.

"No more," he said. "This altitude . . . too much." He turned to me. "Sorry, pumpkin. I'd hoped we could do it. For your ma."

Something about his words made me forget my sore knees. And stand a little taller. "Do you think I could keep going, Pa? Just a little higher? I was hoping, maybe . . . to see a hawk."

He looked at me for a long time. "Well, all right. But see you do just what Mr. Mills says." He gave me a wobbly smile. "Spread your wings, girl. For us all."

For a while, the trail flattened out. Mr. Mills and I hiked through a dark green forest where the air smelled sweet, like vanilla. Fallen needles softened the ground. Then we started up again. My heel got to hurting, and I moved about as slow as a June bug. Mr. Mills asked, "How do you feel, lass?"

"Tell you later."

He put his hand on my head. "Just why do you want to see a hawk?" I didn't answer, and he said, "The summit's where you'll find them, lass. But we must get up there by midafternoon—or we'll never make it back before dark."

My legs moved a bit faster.

Soon my heel hurt worse than ever. Like it was on fire! I leaned against a mossy trunk. Way down below, I could see the trees by the trailhead. Lord, they looked so small! And so far away.

All of a sudden I heard a deep bugling sound. The ground started shaking, rumbling like a thousand drums.

Just then a great bull elk bounded out of the trees, busting through the branches with his rack. He ran right in front of us, followed by a herd of seventy or eighty more.

It took a long while for all those hooves to stop pounding. And even longer for my heart to do the same.

I glanced at Mr. Mills. He winked and said just one word: "Surprises."

As the trail ran past a meadow, Mr. Mills told me how he wanted to make this whole wilderness a national park. "Some say I'm crazy to try," he sighed. "And they're probably right."

I pulled off my boot. A giant blister! Mr. Mills wrapped my foot with his kerchief. "Looks bad, lassie. We should turn back."

"No! I'm not quitting. Not yet, at least." I grabbed my boot and glanced up at the sun. "Let's go. It's past noon already."

His eyebrows lifted. "You're a sturdy lass, you are. And aye, you give me courage for my own climb."

We scrambled up a rocky ridge. The wind howled, and made us lean like broken fence posts. Then we came to a fir tree, standing all by itself. I bent down and touched its twisty roots. And just a little, I smiled. "My ma would've loved this old tree."

Mr. Mills nodded. "You miss her, aye?"

I wanted to answer, but the wind swallowed my words, and made my eyes water.

Higher up, we came to boulders—hundreds of them! All jumbled on top of each other. We had to crawl over them, watching out for sharp points, and cracks so deep I saw no bottom. Sometimes the stones wobbled, rocking like a riverboat. And sometimes my legs wobbled just as much.

Just when I stepped on one boulder, it broke loose. Mr. Mills grabbed my arm. The big rock bounced down the slope and smashed into the stones below. "Is that," I panted, "another one of your surprises?"

Mr. Mills just grinned.

Now came the snow—up to my knees. My feet started hurting again, this time from the cold. And the air felt too thin to breathe. Every so often I looked up, hoping to see a hawk. Just one! But all I saw was the lowering sun.

Then my hair prickled. Mr. Mills yanked me under a lip of rock just as lightning and thunder exploded on top of us. Hail pounded down, bouncing every which way. My teeth kept chattering, even after I ate some of Mr. Mills' shortbread.

Suddenly—the storm stopped. Just like that. Sunlight flashed on the snow, and the whole world sparkled.

Now there was a surprise.

Far as I could see, there was snow. Mr. Mills jumped into it like some kind of mountain goat. "Come on, lass!"

But when I stood, my legs felt stiffer than icicles. I stepped onto a drift and broke right through. Snow was smothering me! Mr. Mills finally hauled me out, but I was shaking like a rattle. And my whole body ached. I shook my head. "Let's g-g-go back."

He shrugged sadly. "All right, lassie. Let's just mount that wee ledge over there before we turn around." I said no—but he'd already started to climb the ledge. Cramped and cold, I hobbled after him, my head hanging low. With frozen fingers, I pulled myself up.

This was no ledge. This was the summit!

Below me stretched a whole world of rock ridges, cloud ridges, and more. A string of lakes, gleaming like a great blue necklace. A sea of endless light, washing over the mountain. And then, soaring out of the sky—a pair of shining wings.

Mr. Mills squeezed me hard. "You did it, lass! So tell me, now. How do you feel?"

I drew a long, slow breath.

"High as a hawk."

Enos Mills with Harriet Peters (age 8) on the summit of Longs Peak, September 1905

Photograph courtesy of the Enos Mills Cabin Collection

From my Colorado home, I can see one mountain rising above the ridge line of the Rockies: Longs Peak. It is with me whatever the season or time of day. Its rosy hues announce the dawn; its slopes form the seam between earth and sky throughout the day; its deepening shadows herald the night. And always, its towering form dominates the surrounding wilderness, the land known as Rocky Mountain National Park.

A few years ago, while researching the life of Enos Mills, the famed mountain guide who founded the park, I came across his file of most cherished letters. He had saved notes from Theodore Roosevelt, John Muir, Helen Keller, Booker T. Washington, John D. Rockefeller, Eugene Debs, Lowell Thomas, Kit Carson—and one eight-year-old girl from Little Rock, Arkansas, named Harriet Peters.

Why, I wondered, among all those letters from the luminaries of his day, did Mills also keep the crumpled, handwritten one from Harriet?

My curiosity sparked, I learned that in September 1905, that very girl had become the youngest person ever to reach the 14,255-foot summit of Longs Peak. Her guide, Enos Mills, was then working hard to protect the mountain and its surroundings for all time, despite fierce opposition from powerful mining and development interests. At that point in time, Mills' goal of a national park seemed impossible to many, just the idealistic dream of one lone homesteader.

I began to wonder what their day together on the mountain had been like. Was it possible that young Harriet had somehow inspired Enos? Had she given him courage to climb his own personal mountain, even as he'd done the same for her? The result is this story. While I have used some poetic license, the story's historical basis in their successful climb is accurate. I am deeply grateful to Enos Mills' daughter, Enda, and his granddaughter, Beth, whose helpfulness made my research both productive and enjoyable. As often happens, the more I learned about the subject, the more I wanted to learn.

Even in the midst of his difficult battle to save the place he loved, Enos Mills found solace—and inspiration—from that mountain he could see from his homestead cabin. And during those years, he continued to prize the memory of his remarkable day with Harriet. He later wrote, "Of the two hundred and fifty-odd trips which I made as a guide to the summit of this great old peak, the trip with Harriet is the one I like best to recall."

Ten years after their climb together, Mills' efforts were finally rewarded when the United States Congress created Rocky Mountain National Park. No doubt he viewed it as a victory not for himself, but for generations to come. And, in particular, for one spunky young girl from Little Rock, Arkansas.

J
PICTURE
E   Barron, T. A.
BAR
High as a hawk.

DATE			